For Theodora —J.O.

For Angie —B.B.

Text copyright © 2014 by Jenny Offill
Jacket and interior illustrations copyright © 2014 by Barry Blitt

Visit us on the Web! randomhouse.com/kids
Educators and librarians, for a variety of teaching tools, visit us at RHTeachersLibrarians.com

Library of Congress Cataloging-in-Publication Data
Offill, Jenny.
While you were napping / Jenny Offill. — 1st ed.
p. cm.
Summary: A child tells an outlandish tale of what took place while a younger sibling was taking a nap.
ISBN 978-0-375-86572-5 (trade) — ISBN 978-0-375-96572-2 (glb) — ISBN 978-0-375-98743-4 (ebook)
[1. Naps (Sleep)—Fiction. 2. Brothers and sisters—Fiction. 3. Humorous stories.] I. Title.
PZ7.O3277Whi 2012
[E]—dc22
2010048532

The text of this book is set in Paradigm.
The illustrations are rendered in pen-and-ink and watercolor.
Book design by Rachael Cole

MANUFACTURED IN CHINA
10 8 6 4 2 1 3 5 7 9
First Edition

While You Were Napping

By Jenny Offill ★ Illustrated by Barry Blitt

schwartz & wade books · new york

Maybe you were right
to scream like you did

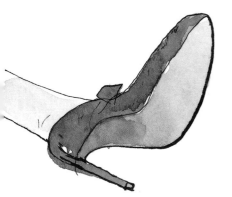

when Mom picked you up
and took you to your bed.

Just a little nap, she said.
You won't miss a thing,
I promise.

And I guess you didn't . . .

. . . unless you count

that giant party that started after she went out.

Nobody else had to take a nap that day,
and we were all playing outside
when a plane appeared and wrote in sky letters:

The construction workers were the first to come.

They were bored with building, they said,

and so they asked all of us kids
to take over their bulldozers for them.

Too bad you were fast asleep,
because you would've liked it, I bet.
Soon we were all ripping up our yards
and hurling dirty dirtballs at our friends.

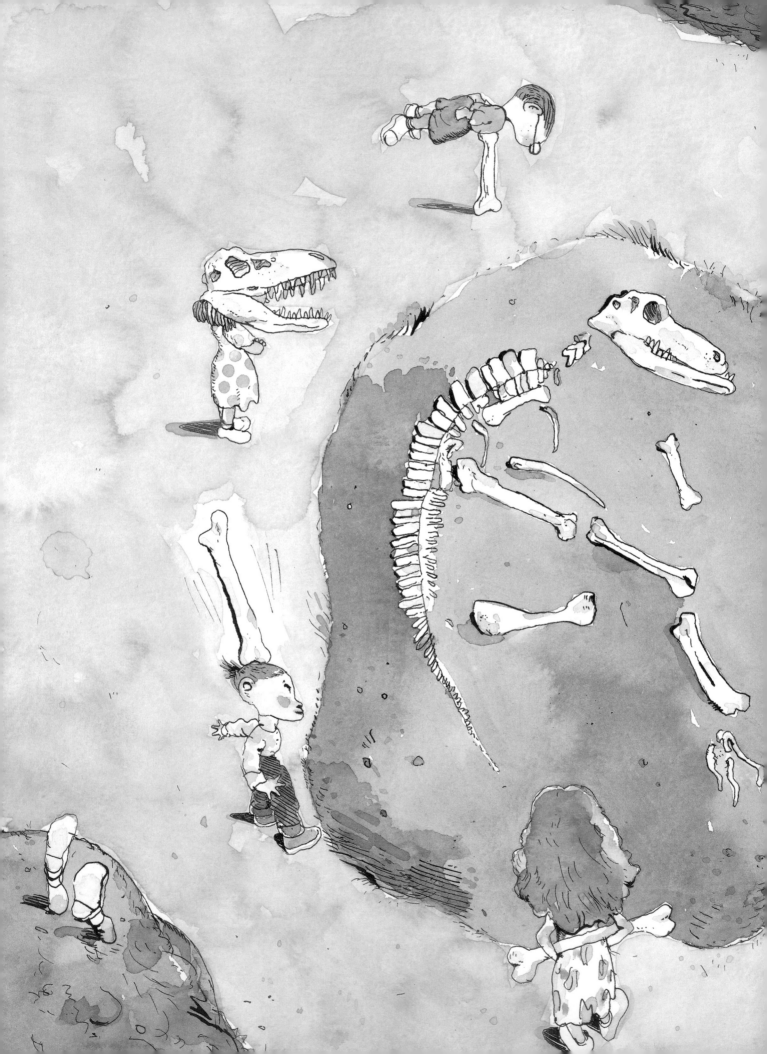

By the time we were done bulldozing,
there was no grass left, only holes,
but then Tommy Binkle found a dinosaur skeleton
and gave each of us a bone.

When the robots came,
they brought cotton candy
(your favorite kind, the blue),

and we all ate as many
french-fry sandwiches as we wanted. And no one made us
say the magic word or asked us to stop drinking the ketchup.

After lunch, it was time for the fireworks.
There were barrels and barrels of them.

And even the littlest babies got to set them off
(as long as they were careful).

I'm pretty sure you would have loved it,

especially when the babies' rockets

made Dad's lawn chair go up in flames

and the firemen raced down our street with their sirens blaring.

We stood so close to the fire
that our eyebrows got a little singed,

and we all took pictures to prove to you
how dangerous it was,
since you were the only kid napping
when it happened.

I guess the pirates must have seen the flames shooting up,
or maybe they heard the sirens,
but they came over right after the firemen left,
with their bandannas and eye patches.

I thought maybe I should wake you up to see them,
but Mom always says never wake a sleeping kid,
so I just went along with the pirates
when they marched us over to Lila Van Wooten's pool.

They lined everyone up on the diving board,
from the bravest to the scaredest,
then waved their big swords in the air
and told us to make our last wishes.

But then we decided not to walk the plank after all
because we didn't have our bathing suits on.

And the pirates were really nice about it
and gave us all peg legs as party favors.

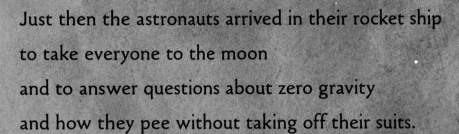

Just then the astronauts arrived in their rocket ship
to take everyone to the moon
and to answer questions about zero gravity
and how they pee without taking off their suits.

It was late by the time we got back from outer space
and shook the moon dust out of our boots.

And we were all a little grumpy,
thinking the fun might have ended.

So we raced around the yard in our underpants
screaming "Blast off!" and "Prepare to die, my friend!"
But luckily we didn't wake you up.

Luckily, you slept right through it.